A Great Trip!

Written by Lauren Robbins

I want to travel everywhere,

On land, on water, in the air.

Ride on a bus across our town.

Get in the subway underground.

Fly on a plane without a care,

And see the whole world from the air.

Ride on a fast train down the track.

Then, turn around and come right back.

Sail on a ship to a faraway land.

Swim and play in the hot, white sand.

Get on a bus, ride on a train,

Fly on a plane, and sail on a ship.

This will be a really great trip.

The only thing I won't do soon,

Is take a rocket to the moon!